Love
from
Louisa

xxx

For
willem
and
Gregor

S.P.

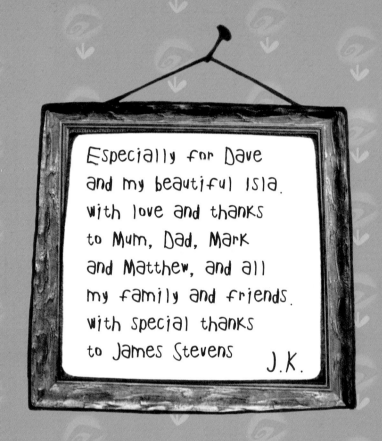

Especially for Dave
and my beautiful Isla.
with love and thanks
to Mum, Dad, Mark
and Matthew, and all
my family and friends.
with special thanks
to James Stevens

J.K.

First published in paperback in Great Britain by HarperCollins Children's Books in 2009

10 9 8 7 6 5 4 3 2

HarperCollins Children's Books is a division of HarperCollins Publishers Ltd.

ISBN-13: 978-0-00-714764-9
ISBN-10: 0-00-714764-3

Text copyright © Simon Puttock 2009
Illustrations copyright © Jo Kiddie 2009

Visit our website at: www.harpercollins.co.uk

Printed by Martins the Printers Ltd

Love from Louisa

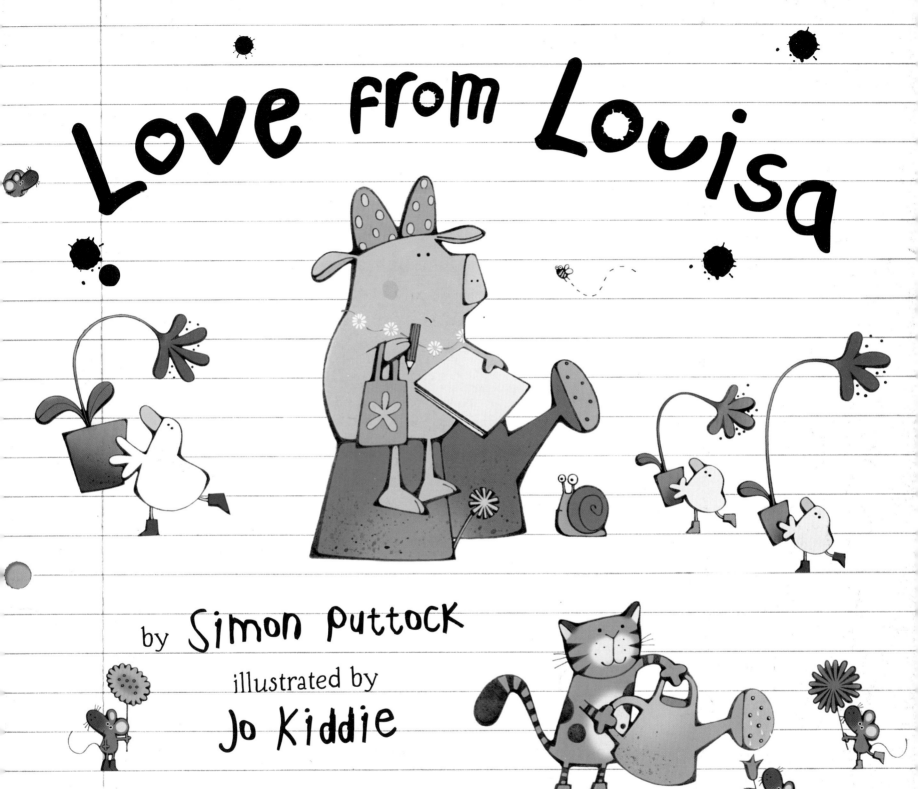

by Simon Puttock

illustrated by Jo Kiddie

HarperCollins *Children's Books*

Louisa the pig was not pleased.
The farm was a mucky mess.
"Something," said Louisa,
"must be done about this."

So she wrote a letter to Farmer Giles.

Dear Farmer Giles,

The farm is mucky and messy. Please clean it up __at once!__

Sincerely,

Disgruntled!

Farmer Giles scratched his head.
Who could the letter be from?
"But whoever it is has a point,"
he remarked. "I'll tidy up a bit."

Farmer Giles mucked out the barn...

cleaned out the henhouse...

Home tweet Home

But Louisa the pig was not impressed. "Huh," she thought, and she wrote another letter.

Dear Farmer Giles,
You have not done enough. <u>Please do more</u>.
Sincerely,
Disgruntled!

...and then he did the pigsty, too. "That," he said, "ought to do it."

Farmer Giles WAS surprised. "Well," he said,
"I suppose I could give the barn a lick of paint."
So the next morning, he got up bright and early
and painted the barn a lovely shade of blue.
Then he painted the henhouse and the pigsty
and his front door, too.

"That's dandy," said Farmer Giles, admiring his handiwork.

the farm

But Louisa the pig did not agree, and she wrote another letter.

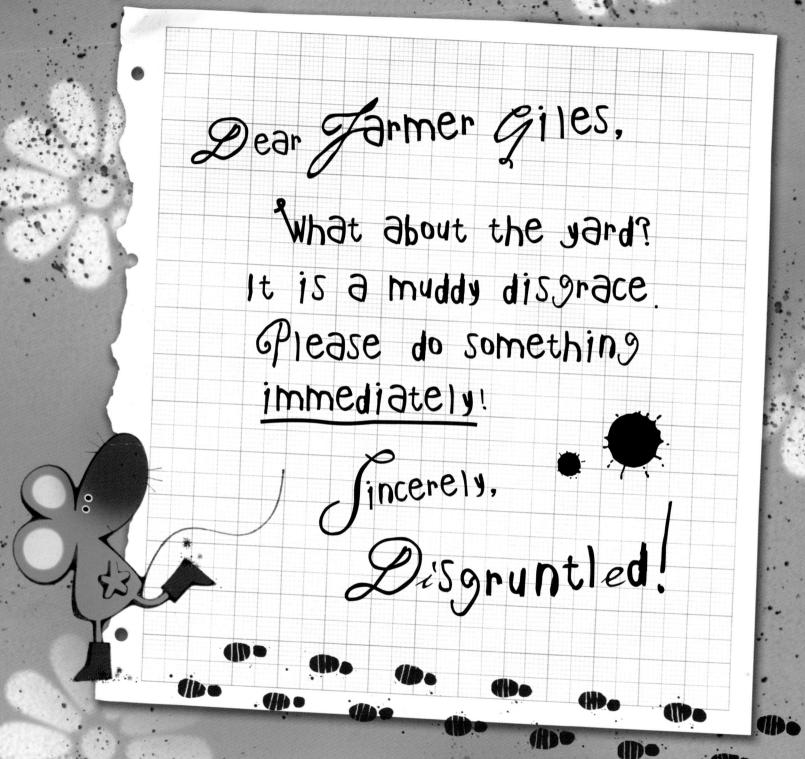

Dear Farmer Giles,

What about the yard?
It is a muddy disgrace.
Please do something
immediately!

Sincerely,

Disgruntled!

Farmer Giles was confounded!
"A barnyard's MADE for mud," he muttered...

Next morning, Farmer Giles
was up before the rooster.

c·o·c·k·a·d·o·o·d·l·e·d·o·o

He got a great big
roller and
rolled...

and rolled...

and rolled the barnyard
until it shone like
chocolate icing.

Louisa the pig just sniffed,
"Mud is such a dreary colour."

Grain

And she wrote another letter.

Dear Farmer Giles,
The farm is now tidy, but it is also very dull.
Please brighten it up. The sooner, the better.
Sincerely,
Disgruntled!

"Whoever can Disgruntled BE?" Farmer Giles wondered.
"But... a bit of colour would cheer the place up."

So next morning,
before the sun had even begun
to rise, Farmer Giles drove into
town and shopped...

and shopped...

and shopped.

Then he took his shopping home and planted it.
The farmyard looked remarkable!
"And THAT," said Farmer Giles, "is THAT!"
But...

Louisa the pig quickly wrote another note.

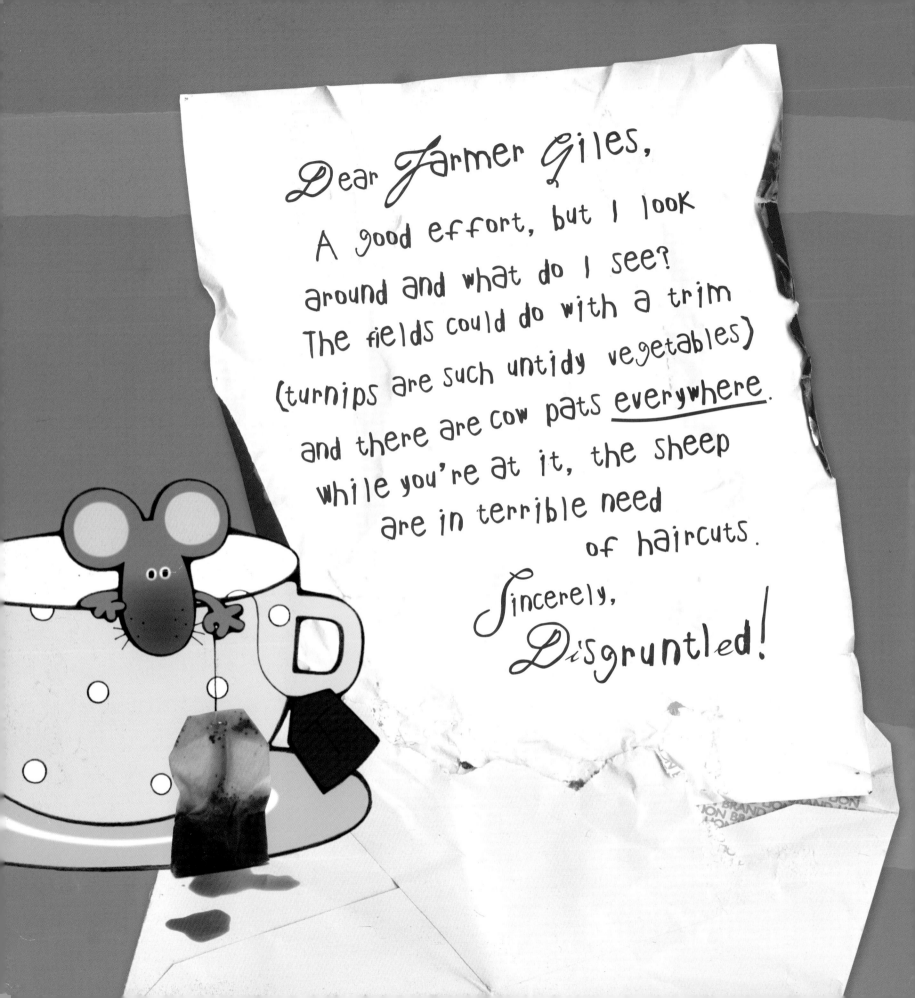

"Enough," shouted Farmer Giles, "is enough! This is a FARM, not a Beauty Parlour!" And he slammed the door and sat down for a sulk.
And while he sulked, it began to rain...

It poured down in bucket and basket and barrel loads. The barnyard got churned, the paintwork got splattered, and the flowers got rained down flat.

"Good grief!" said Farmer Giles.
"There's going to be another horrid letter!"
But then, he had an idea.

He got a great big piece of paper and wrote on it in great big letters:

"Humph!" said Louisa sniffily.
"If that is the way it's going to be,
I shall go SOMEWHERE BETTER!"

She packed her writing things and hitched to the city.

Farmer Giles watched Louisa
driving down the lane.
So THAT was Disgruntled
and she was LEAVING!

"Yahoo!" cried Farmer Giles.
No more annoying letters,
no more daft ideas,
and NO MORE Disgruntled!
"Good riddance to bad rubbish!"

But...

...the city was smoky and smoggy and smelly.
And Louisa wasn't pleased with it at all.

So she wrote another letter.

Dear Farmer Giles,

The city is all very well, but I'm sure you must be missing me terribly. So the good news is, I'm coming home.

Love from Louisa xxx

PS See you soon

And the very next day
she set off...

...back to the farm.